100 Best
After-Dinner
Stories

100 Best After-Dinner Stories

Collected by
PHYLLIS SHINDLER

PIATKUS

It gives me great pleasure to present my third compilation of after-dinner stories and anecdotes by famous and distinguished people from all walks of life.

All the royalties from the book will be devoted to St. Bartholomew's Hospital Children's Cancer Unit, which urgently needs funds to purchase costly medical equipment.

I hope the book will be instructive and amusing for the reader and potential after-dinner speaker.

My grateful thanks to all those distinguished people who took the time and trouble to contribute their stories and anecdotes.

Phyllis Shindler

Copyright © 1992 by Phyllis Shindler

First published in 1992 in
Great Britain by
Judy Piatkus (Publishers) Ltd of
5 Windmill Street, London W1P 1HF

Reprinted 1992 (twice), 1993, 1994

The moral right of the author has been asserted

A catalogue record of this book is available from the British Library

ISBN 0 7499 1189 1
ISBN 0 7499 1183 2 (Pbk)
Illustrations by Ellis Nadler

Typeset in 11/13 Linotron Palatino by
Phoenix Photosetting, Chatham, Kent
Printed and bound in Great Britain by
Mackays of Chatham PLC, Chatham, Kent

Contributors

Foreword
by The Rt. Hon. The Lord Mayor
of London
Sir Brian Jenkins, G.B.E., M.A.

I gladly welcome Mrs. Phyllis Shindler's third compilation of jokes and stories, culled from many people in and around public life, of which, together with her husband, she is a great observer and contributor.

Her previous two books have lent lots of life and laughter to many dire dinners and moody meetings, while raising thousands of pounds for a variety of excellent charitable causes.

For those on the speaking circuit and elsewhere, who have the wit to know that boredom is the great enemy, this latest offering has many weapons of wit to put that enemy to flight.

I wish it the widest possible circulation and the commercial success it deserves in aid of the Children's Cancer Unit at St. Bartholomew's Hospital.

Ted Allbeury
Thriller Writer

Only once in the last five or six years have I indulged
reluctantly in an after-dinner speech, and that was for the
cancer cause in the Channel Islands last year, where I
think the most interesting part of my performance was
that, just before I started talking, my trousers went down
to my ankles.

Peter Alliss

Former Ryder Cup Player
BBC Golf Commentator

Jack Nicklaus was asked by some up and coming young American professionals what would be the best way to tackle the Open Championship which that year was to be played at St. Andrew's. It was their first visit and they'd only read of the trials and tribulations of links golf – how would they cope with the hardness of the ground, the bounce of the ball and the strong winds that blew? Jack went through how to play the pitch and run, using the contours of the ground to smooth the ball in off the banks in an endeavour to get in close to the hole, and was then on the subject of putting in a high wind . . . Of course, he said, one of the main things is to get a really good solid base – wide stance, crouch low over the ball . . . and of course, with the big crowds round the greens they tend to shield you a little from the strong gusts . . . There was a pause, and one of the young professionals said: 'Well, what do you do if there aren't any spectators?' Jack thought for a moment and replied: 'I wouldn't know, I've never played without any spectators!!'

Fiona Armstrong
Television Personality

I introduce myself as Fiona Armstrong – but really, I'm a little confused these days!

Last week I was in a shop, when I saw a lady looking carefully at me. She'd recognised my face, I thought – and true enough, she came across.

'I know who *you* are,' she said. I smiled.

'You're Angela Rippon! Yes, you are, you're Angela Rippon!'

'Really, I'm not!'

'You are! Oh, I shall go and tell everyone I've just met Angela Rippon. How excited I am!'

She disappeared with a smile.

So much for being well-known!

Pamela Armstrong
Journalist and Broadcaster

Jeffrey Archer tells this story against himself.

At the christening of his son, the vicar said: 'May he be blessed with the looks of Mary, and the brains of . . . (pause) Mary.'

Michael Aspel
Television Personality

Rehearsals for *Oedipus* at the National Theatre were going badly. The director, Peter Hall, called the cast to him and told them that he wasn't getting enough fire and passion from them. 'I want you all, one by one, to come on stage and say something – anything – that will really terrify me.'

Each member of the cast stepped forward and roared obscenities and threats into the darkness.

Finally, Sir John (Gielgud) sauntered to the front of the stage, took a languid draw from his cigarette and said:

'We open in two weeks!'

Pam Ayres
Poet, Writer and Journalist

What about this tasteful number? Quite useful, because it can lead on from saying what a delicious dinner we have all just enjoyed, etc:

A lady (or gentleman) had been admitted to hospital but was now recovering nicely. She found that she was looking forward to her lunch and was pleased, as she felt that her returning appetite was a good sign of her improving health. Soon the double doors into the ward opened, and in came the dinner ladies pushing their trolley. She was served with her lunch and enjoyed it mightily. She sat back replete and was having a contented forty winks, when she heard the sound of hurrying feet approaching. The double doors were thrust open, to reveal the desperate faces of the two dinner ladies. Seeing the patient's empty plate waiting for collection, one said to the other: 'Don't tell her now . . . SHE'S *EATEN* IT!'

The Most Reverend Archbishop Luigi Barbarito

Apostolic Pro-Nuncio
Representative of the Pope

It is said that Pope Benedict XIV had a good sense of humour and this lasted until his deathbed.

The story goes that as he lay dying, His Holiness was visited by two Cardinals. They both had reputations for causing him trouble and anxiety, were very critical, and were for ever requesting privileges of one sort or another.

They sat, one on each side of his bed, and attempted to express their grief, as the Pontifical chaplain led the prayers for the dying. At a certain moment there was a sign of revival and the Pontiff woke up and opened his eyes. Everyone listened intently to what he had to say. When he saw that the two Cardinals were with him he uttered a prayer of gratitude: 'I thank you, Lord, that I, like you, am dying between two thieves.'

Adrian Barnes
Remembrancer of the City of London

The French are well known as great sticklers for etiquette and protocol, so I was somewhat apprehensive when conducting a senior French diplomat and her assistant on a lengthy reconnaissance of the Guildhall, prior to a visit by a French President.

Having very carefully explained all the details of the ceremonial: the arrivals, the presentations, the banquet, and so on in almost complete silence, I was told when the recce came to an end: 'Our protocol is older than yours – all this may be changed.'

To which I replied: 'Thank you, Madame, shall we go and have lunch?'

The Rt. Hon. Betty Boothroyd

M.P.

Speaker of the House of Commons

In my early days in politics I was invited as guest speaker to the annual dinner of a local voluntary organisation. Full of chicken and chips and nervous tension, I got through the speech – which I thought had been well received.

On seeing me to my car, the secretary asked, 'And what is your fee?' I was very much taken aback and, somewhat flattered to think I rated a fee. I told the secretary it was a most pleasurable evening for me and there certainly was no fee, to which she replied, 'That's very kind of you, you see we are a new organisation and saving up for a first-class speaker for next year.'

Celia Brayfield
Novelist

This story was told to me on the train from Manchester to London by the actor Joe Melia. We had both been visiting Granada Television and we were really looking forward to getting home. Granada always booked rooms in the Midland Hotel, Manchester, for their guests – a dubious compliment, since the Midland was in those days a byword for its unenlightened style of hospitality. It was the kind of hotel where the maid always left half a teacupful of Vim in the bath, just to reassure you that somebody had cleaned it.

The great comic actor, Arthur Lowe, was staying at the Midland, and came down to eat in the dining-room one evening by himself. Having ordered his meal, he asked the waitress to give him the wine list, which he read through with little enthusiasm.

Not seeing the wine he wanted, he turned to the waitress again and asked, 'Do you have a white Macon?'

'Oh no, sir,' she replied, 'it's just this uniform they make us wear.'

Richard Briers

O.B.E.

Stage, Screen and Television Actor

I went into a Chinese restaurant and I said to the waiter: 'Have you got frog's legs?' He said, 'Yes.' So I said, 'Well hop over the counter and get me a cheese sandwich!'

(Taken from the late Tommy Cooper)

Tony Britton
Stage, Television and Film Actor

Alan Jay Lerner (lyricist of *My Fair Lady*, *Camelot*, *Brigadoon*, *Paint Your Wagon*, etc) told me that at the end of a day's shooting on the Hollywood production of *Brigadoon*, walking across the studio lot he ran into Fred Astaire, exhausted, sweating, a towel slung round his neck, having just finished one of the long, punishing rehearsal sessions he always put himself through when choreographing and practising dances for a movie.

He loped sadly towards Alan with that loose, lanky step, put an arm round his shoulders and asked, 'Why doesn't somebody tell Fred Astaire he can't dance?'

The Reverend David Burgess
Vicar of St Lawrence Jewry Next Guildhall

Parable

The animals met in assembly and began to complain that
humans were always taking things away from them . . .
　'They take my milk,' said the cow.
　'They take my eggs,' said the hen.
　'They take my flesh,' said the pig.
　'They take me for oil,' said the whale.
　And so on . . . until finally the snail spoke: 'I have
something they would certainly take away from me, if
they could. Something they want more than anything
else. I have *time*.'

*　　*　　*

Anecdote

There was a native king in the South Sea Islands who
was giving a banquet in honour of a distinguished guest
from the West. When the time came to praise his guest,
His Majesty remained seated on the floor, while a
professional orator, engaged for the occasion, eulogised
the visitor. After the panegyric, the guest rose to speak.
His Majesty, gently but firmly, held him back. 'Do *not*
stand up.' he said, 'I have engaged an orator for you too
. . . in our island we do *not* leave public speaking to
amateurs!!'

Max Bygraves

O.B.E.
Entertainer and Author

One of my favourite people was the comedian Ted Ray. He was a great raconteur and a sought-after speaker at various functions.

Before he died he passed on a piece of wisdom which I have found beneficial on many occasions. He told me that I might be called upon to speak without warning – people assume that because you are an entertainer you can do it at the drop of a hat. This isn't true; a well-prepared and rehearsed speech is usually best – *but*, if you haven't had time for any preparation, it is second best to 'level' with the audience. Admit it is a surprise but, not to disappoint, add that you will tell *your* favourite half-dozen stories – remembering that nothing is ever old or corny if done with charm and sincerity. You will sit down to generous applause . . .

I usually start with this one:

The Gulf War is on, and two fellows go by on a floating carpet. 'Shoot it down!' says Saddam Hussein.

'I don't think we should,' says the tank commander, 'it's an Allied Carpet!!!'

Follow with your top stories.

The Most Reverend and Rt. Hon. Dr. George Carey

D.D., M.Th., Ph.D.

Archbishop of Canterbury

A preacher was notoriously boring. One Sunday, the verger tried a little experiment to liven up the sermon – he laced the vicar's water with gin. The sermon that followed was remarkable. It was funny, down-to-earth, full of neat illustrations, hard-hitting and spiritually enlightening. The parishioners were astonished and the verger was jubilant.

The next Sunday, he stepped up the gin in the water and another sensational sermon followed, even more powerful than the last.

On the third Sunday, the bishop was visiting the church, so, in honour of this occasion, the verger put nine-tenths gin to one-tenth water. The vicar excelled himself, preaching on the story of Daniel in the Lion's Den. The pulpit shook as he paced up and down, he acted the parts, he laughed, he cried, he shouted, he whispered, he touched the hearts of his congregation, he fired their enthusiasm, he inspired them to follow Daniel's example. After the service, the bishop shook the vicar's hand warmly.

'A very good sermon,' he told him, 'but there's only one small point. God sent an angel to shut the mouths of the lions. Daniel didn't "zap them between the eyes and strew their brains across the walls like spaghetti."'

Patrick Cargill
Actor and Television Personality

In the early Seventies, I was wandering along
Shaftesbury Avenue when a man about my age stopped
short as he saw me, hesitated a moment and then said:
'Isn't it Patrick Cargill?' 'Yes,' I said, 'it is.' 'Good
Heavens!' he retorted. 'Surely you remember me?' I
didn't, of course, and dithered. He helped me out.
'Michael Sudbury – Haileybury – 1931.' 'Good gracious!' I
pretended. 'Well, well, well.' Minor pleasantries
followed, and we repaired to a nearby bar.

Over our beers I did manage to get some slight
recollection of our association at school, and was
delighted to recall that we both had a mutual friend,
Charlie . . . something-or-other. 'Charlie,' I said, in
triumph. 'Now he was a lad! I wonder what became of
him?' Michael's face fell. 'Oh, haven't you heard?' he
said sadly. 'Dead, poor chap.' 'Oh, no!' I replied,
assuming rather more distress than I actually felt.

'Well,' continued Michael, 'you know what a madcap
he was. One day, it appears, he was in Paris, walking
across a bridge over the Seine – can't be content with the
pavement of course, has to walk on the parapet – misses
his footing, slips and falls. There was a steamer passing
underneath and he went straight down the funnel.'

In a flash, the whole fantastic picture swept into my
mind, and I envisaged every comic I had ever known
doing exactly the same thing. The result was that I
shrieked with uncontrollable laughter.

Michael was deeply shocked. 'I suppose you do realise
he's DEAD, don't you?' 'Yes,' I said, tears of laughter
welling into my eyes. 'It's just that I can't help finding
the mental picture unbelievably funny.' And another
regrettable guffaw emitted.

Michael found it quite impossible to understand my
reaction. 'I am totally appalled at your behaviour!' he

said. 'I would have thought a man of your standing would have a little more sensitivity.' And with that, he slammed his glass on the table, strode out of the bar, and I have never seen or heard of him since!

Harry Carpenter
Television Sports Commentator

I spent several years in the TV golf commentary box with the late Henry Longhurst, the doyen of golf writers and commentators. In 1968, the first year BBC Television went into colour, I started wearing gaudy ties in the mistaken belief that as we were now in colour, one should dress colourfully.

At the end of the day, Henry laid an avuncular hand on my arm and said quietly: 'Now, Harry, I have been gazing at that tie of yours. You must tell me . . . are those your old school colours – or your own unfortunate choice?'

B. J. Clayton

F.S.V.A., J.P.
Specialist in Fine Arts

Case in the Magistrates' Court

Solicitor for the Defence: 'My client wishes to apologise, your Worships, for the rather unfortunate state of his driving licence. It was left in his trouser pocket and has been subjected to the entire automatic programme of his mother's washing machine.'

Clerk of the Court (quite oblivious): 'The defendant produces a clean licence, your Worships.'

Group Captain John Constable

B.A., F.C.I.S., F.Inst.A.M., F.B.I.M.

Secondary and Under-Sheriff of the Central Criminal Court

Judge (on seeing a very familiar face appear in the dock): 'Jones, aren't you ashamed to be seen yet again in this place?'

Jones: 'What's good enough for you, M'Lord, is good enough for me.'

His Honour Judge Coombe

Central Criminal Court
Old Bailey

It was a hot summer's day at the Old Bailey. The jury
included two particularly pretty girls in the front row.
Imaginative, if eccentric, Counsel for the Defence began
his speech this way: 'Members of the Jury, I want you to
join me on this hot day. Take off every stitch of clothing.
I will do the same, and together we will plunge into a
cooling sea of sweet reason.'

The pretty jurors lowered their eyes.

Judge: 'Mr——, the jury and I do not accept your
           invitation.'

Counsel: 'You, my Lord, are not invited.'

May I add that I was not the Judge concerned!

Henry Cooper

O.B.E.

Former Champion Heavyweight Boxer

I was travelling up to Glasgow, Scotland, to play golf with the late Graham Hill who was flying me up in his plane, which was plastered with adverts for a tobacco company, and the plane was nicknamed 'The flying cigarette packet.'

Graham said to me: 'How high would you like me to fly the plane?' I said: 'Three foot six inches, because that's my inside leg measurement and, if necessary, I can jump out.'

Jilly Cooper
Author, Journalist and Television Personality

My lovely secretary was telling me that when she was about twenty-eight, her six-year-old daughter came rushing into the house from school and said: 'Mummy, mummy, we were learning about the olden days today. You know the olden days, when Jesus was alive and you were a little girl.'

Ronnie Corbett

O.B.E.

Actor, Comedian and Television Personality

This joke concerns a chap who is working late one night in the office with his gorgeous blonde secretary. And as they're just finishing the paperwork, the secretary leans across the desk and says: 'Mr. Masterson . . . (sigh) . . .' Because she got out of breath very easily, this girl. A bit like my Uncle Sid who has a lot of difficulty breathing these days. He's dead. No, he isn't. That's just a story he puts around to gain sympathy. She says, 'It's very late, Mr. Masterson, don't you think it's time we were both in bed?' Well, being something of an opportunist, this chap didn't need to stick his finger out of the window to see which way the wind was blowing, so he ends up back at her place and a good time is had by all. Especially him. Well, eventually, he looks at his watch and says, 'My God, my wife'll kill me.' So he quickly gets dressed and is about to rush off, when the girl says, 'Hang on, there's nothing to worry about. Just put this bit of chalk behind your ear, tell your wife exactly what happened, and you'll be fine.' So off he goes, gets home, and there is his wife, sitting up in bed, sharpening the kitchen knife on her tongue. She says, 'Where the hell have you been?' So, remembering what he's been told, the chap says, 'Well, dear, I was working late with my beautiful secretary Fiona, and I'm afraid she invited me back to her flat and one thing led to another, and I ended up being unfaithful to you.' At which point the wife suddenly notices the piece of chalk sticking out behind his ear and says, 'You ruddy liar, don't give me that – you've been down the pub again, playing darts.'

Colin Cowdrey

C.B.E.

Former Captain of England and of Kent County
Cricket Club
Former Master of the Worshipful Company of Skinners

On my first tour of Australia in 1954, I had the luck to hit
form and score 100 in the first innings against New South
Wales. Whilst we were fielding, we ran into some
injuries and, as we walked off the field just after tea, the
captain, Len Hutton, asked me whether I would open the
innings with Reg Simpson of Nottinghamshire. It was a
nerve-racking moment, but I was able to cling on, and
by the close of play I was 80 odd not out and within sight
of notching a coveted hundred in each innings, which
does not happen very often in a career.

The next morning I overslept, was awakened by those
going to the ground and had to make a mad dash. As I
ran from the lift to the waiting car, the hall porter of the
hotel thrust a telegram into my hand. In my nervousness
I opened it, cast my eye over it two or three times, could
make neither head nor tail of it and thrust it in my
pocket, exclaiming: 'Crank!'

I had the excitement of scoring my second hundred,
the game went the full distance and we went straight
from the ground to the airport to catch a plane to
Brisbane, and into bed very late at night. As I was
undressing, I found the crumpled telegram which read:
'Two kings thirty-nine seventeen.'

As I stared at it, I realised it could be a reference to the
Old Testament, second book of Kings, chapter thirty-
nine, verse seventeen. I opened up the Bible and there it
was – a message meant for me: 'And the Lord said to
Elijah, do it the second time.'

Sadly, it had been sent to me without any name and
address, and I was not able to share the fun of receiving
it and the good luck that it brought me.

Happily, when I travelled with England to Australia two tours and eight years later, I was telling this story in an interview on Australian radio. An hour later, there was a telephone call from the original sender who lived 600 miles up country. It was good to be able to thank the lady for her special message and we were able to have a laugh about it all.

Susan Crosland
Novelist and Journalist

Next door to me in Kensington lives an independent-minded elderly widow. She has a fondness for the bottle, and takes pleasure in quietly drinking throughout the day. Maintained by her own vast inherited fortune, she harms no one by her little habit. Yet her four middle-aged children decided bossily on what is currently known as 'loving intervention.'

Just before dawn, they arrived (complete with spouses) before their mother had woken, much less had a cup of coffee. 'Mother, we've come to talk with you. Now who will speak first?'

When each of the gang had spoken, one then said: 'Mother, it's entirely up to you. We can take you to the clinic now.' The old lady replied that she would prefer to disinherit her children.

The moral of the story appears to be: mind your own business. But in this instance there was a further sting in the tail for the disinherited children. The youngest son, who had been the actual instigator of this 'loving intervention', happened to be called abroad on business at the last minute. Thus he was not with his siblings on that fateful morning when they marched *en masse* into their mother's bedroom. She has left her entire fortune to him.

Leslie Crowther
Television Personality and Presenter

Here is a Grace which is very apt for a stag dinner:

> We bless your Miracle divine
> Of turning water into wine;
> Now please forgive we foolish men
> Who seem to turn it back again!

Also, an American poem some speakers might do well to take to heart:

> I love a finished speaker,
> I really truly do;
> I don't mean one who's polished,
> I just mean one who's through.

Edwina Currie

M.P.

Former Parliamentary Undersecretary of State for Health

The afternoon of the adoption meeting started well enough at a local school. I parked the big Citroën, my husband's pride and joy and lent to me only while my battered Austin was being serviced. I spent a happy hour inside at the meeting and returned – to find the car gone.

'Was that your blue car which ran off down the road?' asked a lady. 'It ran down into Mr. Theaker's garden and knocked down his wall,' she said helpfully. 'He's hopping mad.'

Down the road I went. It had started to rain. Mr. Theaker was indeed standing in the demolished remains of his garden, wagging his finger: 'Shan't vote for you,' he said. But where was the car? And what state was it in? Was I about to lose my husband's vote as well as Mr. Theaker's?

And so to Swadlingcote police station, where three straight-faced sergeants solicitously asked about my relationship with my husband: 'Get on well, do you? That's lucky.' . . . I was getting panicky, and at last they took pity on me and escorted me to a nearby breaker's yard, where the forlorn-looking car stood with only one headlight broken. The locals have been teasing me about this runaway start to our campaign ever since.

Les Dawson

Comedian, Television Personality and Author

A duck went into a chemist's shop and said, 'Could I
have a tube of Lipsyl please?'
   The chemist said, 'Certainly – that will be 50p.'
   And the duck said, 'Well put it on my bill.'

*   *   *

An old lion tamer got careless, and one of the lions bit his
ear off. They rushed him to hospital and managed to sew
a pig's ear on to replace his own. Someone asked him a
month later: 'What's your hearing like now?' He said:
'Not too bad; my own ear is fine – but I get crackling in
the new one.'

General Sir Peter de la Billiere

K.C.B., C.B.E., D.S.O., M.C.

Commander of H.M. Forces in the Gulf War

The times were when gay people were happy, queer people were distinctly odd, and only Generals had Aides.

The Rt. Hon. Lord Denham

P.C., K.B.E.

Former Government Chief Whip, House of Lords
Author

During the First World War, an officer in the trenches
received, sent out from England, a birthday present
which was what he wanted more than anything else, a
small barrel of real draft bitter beer. He took it along to
the Mess where, with great ceremonial, the bung and tap
were inserted and it was left to stand and settle for two
days. On the day of his birthday, with equal ceremonial
and mounting excitement, he drew his first pint. To his
and his friends' utter disappointment, it was absolutely
filthy. They were about to throw the whole thing out into
no-man's-land in disgust, when somebody had an idea.
The sergeants in that particular battalion were reputed to
be able to drink anything. Why not send it along to
them? And this, accordingly, they did. The next day the
officer approached his own platoon sergeant with a
certain amount of apprehension, and the conversation
went as follows:

'Did you have any of that beer last night, Sergeant
Jones?'

'Yes, Sir.'

'What was it like?'

'It was just right, Sir.'

'Just right? How do you mean?'

'Well, Sir, if it had been any worse we couldn't have
drunk it and if it had been any better we wouldn't have
got it.'

His Honour Judge Denison
Central Criminal Court

I have always liked the story (true) about F. E. Smith as a young barrister (he later became Lord Chancellor). He was arguing a point of law before a rather testy judge who, after some time, said: 'Mr. Smith, I have listened to you for twenty minutes and I am no wiser.' F. E. responded: 'Your Lordship may well be no wiser, but your Lordship is certainly better informed.'

*   *   *

I also fancy the story (not true) of the Englishman who arrived at Sydney, Australia, tired after a long flight. He had to queue for immigration, and by the time he was questioned by the immigration officer, he was feeling decidedly irritated. His temper got worse during the lengthy interrogation, so that when he was asked, 'Do you have any criminal convictions?' he replied, 'I didn't know you still needed them to enter Australia.'

Ted Dexter

Chairman of the England Cricket Selectors
Former Captain of England and Sussex

I was feeling self-important as the newly appointed
Chairman of the England Cricket Committee, expecting
instant recognition. However, trying to enter Lord's at
the Grace Gate, my face, my smart suit and my polished
car cut little ice, until I was forced to give my full name
and title.

My sense of triumph at being waved through was
deflated when I overheard the gateman grumbling to his
assistant: 'I hope he knows where to find him.'

His Excellency M. Bernard Dorin

Ambassador of France

Do you know the difference between a Diplomat and a Lady?

When a Diplomat says 'yes', it means 'maybe'; if he says 'no', he is not a Diplomat.

When a Lady says 'no', she means 'maybe'; if she says 'yes', she is not a Lady.

I leave it to you to guess what happens when a Diplomat meets a Lady!

Hugh Dykes

M.P.

Former Chairman of Conservative Group for Europe

A certain very bossy and much-disliked Governor's wife, at a reception one night sent the ADC to enquire the name of a tune which the band was playing, and to which she had taken a fancy.

The ADC went, and on returning she said to him: 'Captain Smith, what was the tune called?' At that moment there was a dead silence throughout the room, and in ringing and soldierly tones the ADC was heard to say: 'You will remember my kisses, Madame, when I have forgotten your name.'

Michael Fish

Meteorologist, Television Personality and Weather Presenter

A colleague in the old days of magnetic rubber was showing foggy weather, when the letter 'F' dropped off. He ignored it until the end, when he said, 'Thank you, goodnight – sorry about the "F" in "fog".'

Frederick Forsyth
Author of *The Day of the Jackal* and other best selling books

During a long and tiring train journey, three men – an Englishman, a Frenchman and a Russian – came into conversation which soon turned to the ultimate definition of absolute happiness. The Englishman had no doubts:

'I am sitting in the library of my Wiltshire manor house. The light from a roaring log fire falls upon rows of leather-bound books left to me by my forefathers. I have had an excellent supper of cold roast beef and a glass of claret stands at my elbow. The servants have gone to their quarters, my wife is visiting her parents, my trusty gun dog lies at my feet. Some good, light classical music envelopes me from the music centre. I have had a superb day fishing for salmon and I shall have an excellent day shooting pheasants tomorrow. Contentment is total. This, my friends, is true happiness.'

The Frenchman shook his head vigorously:

'No, my friends, true happiness is quite different. As for me, I am sitting at my favourite window table in the Tour d'Argent, looking out at the illuminations of my beloved Paris. A sumptuous meal is being prepared for me. At my left hand sits a stunning blonde and to my right an amazing brunette. A Château Mouton Rothschild is breathing in the decanter, the night ahead can only be completely fulfilling – that, I suggest, is true happiness.'

Both men waited for the Russian, who finally shook his head and gave his own definition:

'I am in my tiny, overcrowded and jerry-built Moscow apartment. I am in my shirtsleeves and braces, watching Moscow Dynamo knock seven bells out of Spartak. Suddenly there is a ring at the door. I rise, go out into the hall and peer through the keyhole. Outside are two men in grey raincoats, clearly KGB. Behind them are four armed and uniformed KGB guards. With a sigh, I return to the sitting-room; I kiss my trusty and loyal wife Ludmilla for the last time, urge my son Boris to stick to his studies, embrace my daughter Tanya and bid her look after her mother in the years to come. Finally I take my jacket, my hat and my coat (for it will be cold in Siberia) and open the door. The senior KGB man says, "Petrov, you are under arrest, come with us." I reply, "I am Kukushkin – Petrov lives upstairs." And that, my friends, is the meaning of real happiness.'

The Rt. Hon. Lord Forte

F.R.S.A., F.B.I.M.

Chairman of Trusthouse Forte Ltd.
Hon. Consul-Gen. of San Marino

The Good Book allots us a share of life of three score years and ten . . . and here I am already showing a handsome 14.3 per cent on the deal. (On his 80th birthday.)

Hannah Gordon
Actress and Television Personality

Some years ago I was on location for a film in a town in Lancashire. The director had selected a house at the end of a terrace in a typical north country street that was to appear as the exterior of the studio set in which most of the action took place. The lady who answered the door to the location manager when he went to ask her permission for us to work there was very amenable, particularly when a location fee was mentioned.

Everything went well with the arrangements, when we would hope to be there and for how long, etc – until she asked how many people would be involved. The location manager said, 'Well . . . it's a full unit; cameras, sound and all that. I suppose it would be about sixty people, counting the drivers and everyone.' Her face fell – 'Oh dear, I couldn't manage that, I'm afraid . . . I've only got eight cups.'

Sir Alexander Graham

G.B.E., D.C.L.

Lord Mayor of London, 1990–91

A visiting preacher at Sunday Chapel at Eton was carefully instructed that he must not let the sermon go on for longer than ten minutes, as that was the outside limit for retaining the attention of the boys.

When he finally sat down, having preached for some fifteen minutes, the Chaplain got up and announced the next hymn.

'We will now sing Hymn number 283, omitting verses 1, 2, 3, 4 and 5. Let us pray!'

*　　　*　　　*

A Sunday School teacher sent her pupils away and told them to come back the following Sunday with something to represent a story from the Bible.

The next Sunday only three had remembered to bring anything:

Sarah came clutching a toy lamb. 'What do you represent?' said the teacher. 'I am the Good Shepherd,' answered Sarah. 'Excellent,' said the teacher. 'Have some Smarties.'

Julian was next – I didn't know Julian was a name until I visited Eton where everyone was a Julian! He held a candle, wax up to his elbows, wax dripping on his shoes and on his face – a terrible mess. 'What are you?' said the teacher. 'I am the light of the world,' replied Julian. 'Excellent,' said the teacher. 'Have some moon dust.' – Revolting stuff, it really should carry a government health warning.

James came last, holding a lollipop. The teacher dredged her memory of the Bible but could think of no reference to a lollipop – she thought it must have been in the Apocrypha and she was not good on the Apocrypha.

'Well, what are you?' she said. James replied, 'Hold fast to all things that are good.'

Rosemary Harris
Author of Fiction, Thrillers and Children's Books

A well-known and wealthy woman, troubled by vague
pains in her chest, went to see a doctor who, after
examining her, shook his head gravely and said that her
condition was such that he must have a second opinion –
he would make an appointment and give her a note to
take with her to the specialist. She went home, put it on
the mantelpiece, and sat looking at it day after day, torn
with anxiety. At last the strain was too great and she
couldn't resist tearing open the envelope. The note was
brief. It read: 'Dear Bill, I am sending you a fine fat
pigeon for your plucking. When you have finished with
her, make sure you send her back to me.'

*   *   *

There was an old woman who lived in a shoe.
She had so many children she didn't know what to do –
presumably.

Sarah Harrison
Writer

A friend of mine is an inveterate – and involuntary – Spooneriser. At a time when he and his wife were living in Kent, not far from Chartwell, they were regular Saturday morning customers at a nearby coffee house noted for its tranquillity and period charm. One weekend they had an important US business associate staying, and took him to the coffee house at the usual time. The elderly waitress approached their table and my friend gave their order, concluding with: 'And I'll have my usual – an espresso and one of your largest cock-rakes.'

Bernard P. Harty

I.P.F.A., M.B.C.S.
Chamberlain of the City of London Corporation

A Corporation in a certain country was adjudged to have failed the nation. The chief executive, finance director, and engineering director were each sentenced to death by guillotine; that bloody blade which this year celebrates its bicentenary.

On the appointed day, before a great crowd, the chief executive put his head on the block and the lever was pulled. But the blade did not fall. The law of the land forbade a second try, and the chief executive walked away, a free man.

The finance director went next. Again, the lever was pulled and, again, unaccountably, the blade failed to fall, and the finance director also was freed.

Then came their remaining colleague. The engineering director put his head upon the block; as the lever was about to be pulled, he looked up and called out, 'Wait a minute! I can see what's wrong.'

The Rt. Hon. Sir Edward Heath

K.G., P.C., M.B.E., M.P.
Former Prime Minister

While Minister of Labour for Great Britain, I had the pleasure to have a meeting with President Khrushchev of the Soviet Union. While discussing relations between our two countries, Mr. Khrushchev bluntly stated that Britain must do more trade with the Soviet Union and that we must buy more Russian goods, if trade relations were to be enhanced.

I replied, 'Yes, I agree, but I have trouble getting the British people to buy British goods, let alone Russian! Besides, what is it that we could buy from you?'

He staunchly answered, 'Well, you could buy Russian watches.'

'Russian watches!' I replied in amazement. 'Whatever for?'

With amusement, he answered, 'Well, Russian watches are cheaper than Swiss watches, they are of better quality, they are more accurate, and they go faster!'

The late Benny Hill

Comedian and Television Personality

Six Hell's Angels went into a bar and started picking on this little chap. They pulled his hair, poured his beer over him and pushed him about. The little chap paid his bill and departed.

One Hell's Angel said to the barman, 'He's not much of a man, letting us do that to him.' The barman said, 'He's not much of a driver, either. He's just backed his truck over six brand new motorbikes!'

Jimmy Hill
Television Sports Commentator and Sportsman

A theatre critic was writing about a pantomime which was particularly horrific.

'In conclusion,' he wrote, 'it appears to me that this is a particularly ungenerous review and that I have knocked everything, except the chorus girls' knees; but sadly the Almighty beat me to it!'

Bob Holness
Television and Radio Personality, Presenter of
Blockbusters

Being a good game-show host necessitates getting to know your contestants, and I do spend a lot of time discovering their hobbies and interests. It makes all the difference when they win a prize they really want and can make use of. There was one occasion, though, when the contestant went green when awarded a trip to a sub-aqua diving school, which had been specially organised for him. It was so obviously the wrong choice – and he showed it – that we had to stop recording.

'What's the matter?' I asked. 'Didn't you say that you like diving lessons?'

'No,' he trembled . . . 'I said DRIVING lessons; I suffer from hydrophobia!!'

The Rt. Hon. Denis Howell

M.P.

Former Minister of Sport

When I entered Parliament in 1955, I was already well known as a Football League referee. As a result of my becoming a Member of Parliament, I became known as the M.P. Referee. This often caused some amusing incidents and it was, of course, a natural source of ammunition for spectators who wished to have a go at me.

I was refereeing a match one day at Swindon and had to give a lot of decisions against the home side, which finally resulted in an outburst of booing directed towards me. When the noise had ceased, there was just one moment of silence, such as you get on great sporting occasions, when a lone voice could be heard from the back of the terraces directed at me with his great insult. 'It's about time they sent you to the Lords!'

Unfortunately, my critic was too far away from me to hear my reply, which was to the effect: 'I am afraid the Prime Minister (Harold Wilson) does not always accept the advice offered to him, and certainly won't in this case.'

Sir Peter Imbert

Q.P.M.

Commissioner of the Metropolitan Police

I recall the day in 1985 when I arrived at New Scotland Yard for my first day as the newly appointed Deputy Commissioner. My ex-Royal Marine driver, wearing a smart police uniform, jumped out of the car, saluted the patrolling police officer outside Scotland Yard, and announced: 'The new Deputy Commissioner reporting for duty.' To which the Yard man saluted back and said: 'I am very pleased to meet you, Sir, but who is the little man at the back?'

Sir Bernard Ingham

Former Chief Press Secretary to Mrs Thatcher 1979–90
Journalist

Picture the scene. Mrs. Thatcher and Mr. Gorbachev emerging from supper during the interval of *Swan Lake* at the Bolshoi in Moscow, during her highly successful visit before the 1987 general election. They are in animated conversation and great good humour after a somewhat lingering supper. With a colleague, I seek to inform her that the audience has been sitting in the dark for a good ten minutes, waiting for the curtain to go up – or, more accurately, for Mr. Gorbachev and Mrs. Thatcher to return to their box so that the performance may continue.

Mrs. Thatcher introduces me to Mr. Gorbachev as the man who keeps the British press in order. Mr. Gorbachev retorts: 'But I thought you said your press were independent?' Mrs. Thatcher looks to me for help. 'Altogether too independent for my liking, sir,' I reply. Mr. Gorbachev roars his way back to his box in even better humour.

Derek Jacobi

C.B.E.

Star of Stage, Screen and Television

The Duke of Windsor, when Prince of Wales, visited a northern town and attended a dinner in his honour. The Mayor, after a paean of praise about the Prince, turned to his surprised fellow guests with the words: 'If you'd do what 'e do you wouldn't do what you do do.' Bad advice as it turned out!

*   *   *

Sir Winston Churchill was a member of Trinity House. He went to France for a special occasion, dressed in the Trinity House uniform, which puzzled the French. One Frenchman plucked up courage to ask Sir Winston what the uniform was he was wearing. Sir Winston said: 'I am an elder brother of the Trinity.' To which the astonished Frenchman replied: 'MON DIEU!'

Lord Jakobovits
Emeritus Chief Rabbi

Three men, who had been doomed by their doctors to die within three months, were asked how they would spend the time left to them. The Scotsman answered that he would cheerfully squander his savings on all the pleasures he had previously denied himself. The Frenchman spoke of the utter abandon with which he would dine and wine to his heart's content. And the Jew simply said, 'I would look for another doctor to get a second opinion.'

I used this story not only to launch my homiletical ship of solemn exhortation with the merry champagne of a little laughter, but also to illustrate the perennial refusal of the Jew to regard anything as final or inevitable. Whenever in our long history others forecast the doom of Jewry, writing off Jewish survival, or talked, in the diabolical language of the Nazis, of 'the Final Solution' of the Jewish problem, the Jew – refusing to accept finality – always consulted his faith for a second opinion.

Glenys Kinnock

Chair of the overseas development agency, One World
Action
Part-time Teacher

Cardiganshire people are known to be very 'careful' with
money. So much so that, on a very fine day last summer,
a man painting the upstairs windows of his home in
Aberystwyth pulled out his handkerchief to mop his
brow, and a 10p piece left his pocket with it. He slid
down the ladder to recover the 10p – just in time for it to
hit him on the head.

The Rt. Hon. Neil Kinnock

M.P.

Former Leader of the Opposition

A canvasser asked a tired-looking woman with a child in a shawl, two other little ones hanging on her skirt, a large bag of potatoes and another of laundry, how she was going to vote.

'I don't know until I've asked my husband,' said the woman.

The campaigner was appalled and went on to a sermon about the woman's rights and the need to have her own opinion and use her own vote.

'Oh, I know all about that,' said the woman. 'But voting is the only thing my husband ever does for himself so I let him get on with it.'

Prue Leith
O.B.E.
Cookery Expert

I try not to speak after dinner, having once shared a platform with Jeffrey Archer. I was due to give the five-minute 'reply for the guests', at one of those mammoth Grosvenor House banquets, with a top table and 1400 guests, for the Bacon and Pigmeat Federation, or some such. Jeffrey Archer (who was then Vice-Chairman of the Tory Party) was to do the main speech, inspiring the bacon-men to ever better efforts for the country's sake.

But just as the pipers were trying to pipe the top table into the room, Jeffrey said, 'I'm doing the "five-minute" funny at the end, am I not?' Whereupon a desperate debate took place, with the poor organisers pointing to the printed programme announcing Jeffrey Archer as main speaker, and me protesting that I'd worked hard on being jolly for five minutes and could not possibly be serious for twenty instead, and Jeffrey saying, 'Oh nonsense, Prue knows much more about bacon than I do. And besides, I've given eleven proper speeches this week and I'm not doing another one, and besides, if you insist you will hear from my agents in the morning, and besides, I'm the funniest speaker in the country, and Prue could not possibly follow me.' At this point, to my utter astonishment, I heard myself say, 'Oh, all right, all right, I'll do it,' and in we went.

I then spent a miserable dinner trying to write a speech on the back of a menu with an eyebrow pencil. I did have the slight satisfaction of telling the audience, when the evil hour came, that the reason I was on my feet and Jeffrey Archer was not, was because he'd flatly refused to make the speech.

But the awful fact is that he was right. I could not possibly have followed his speech. When he did get up to do the reply for the guests, he started, 'Well, as the

Polish Ambassador is sitting on my left, I cannot possibly tell the story of the Polack who . . .' and then he told us a Polish joke, and the banqueting room rocked with mirth. Then he said, 'As the Irish Minister is present I cannot tell you about Paddy and Spud . . .' and then we got, 'As the South African Ambassador is here I cannot tell you the one about Little Black Sambo . . .' – and so on, until he'd done every racist joke in the book. Finally, he said, 'And as Prue is the only woman in the room I cannot possibly tell you the story of the woman who had the largest . . .' – and then he told a joke that was so blue I simply could not understand it.

The bacon exporters loved him. They fell about. They roared, they clapped, and I resolved never to make after-dinner speeches.

The Rt. Hon. Sir Nicholas Lyell

Q.C., M.P.

The Attorney General

One of my favourite stories is a moral tale, whose moral is not only apposite to politicians.

It was a reminiscence of Mr. Khrushchev when he was a boy, walking in the woods one winter's day near Moscow.

As he made his way through the pines and silver birches, he came to a ride. Suddenly he saw a poor injured bird fleeing from the undergrowth, chased by a hungry fox. Being a compassionate spirit, he drove the fox away and rescued the bird, cradling it in his hands for warmth. He was wondering what to do with it when, as luck would have it, a horse trotted by and, as horses are wont to do, left a pile of droppings in the ride. Seeing the steaming mound, a thought came to him and, taking a small stick, he made a hole in the pile, placed the bird gently in it and went on his way.

The creature, which had been more harmed by the cold than injured, benefited from the warmth and restoring vapours, popped his head up above the mound and began to sing. Whereupon the hungry fox came out of the woods again and ate it up.

There are two morals to this tale. Neither is exclusively relevant to politicians. The first is, that it is not only your enemies who may drop you in it. The second is, that if you are in it up to your neck, keep your mouth shut!

*   *   *

Another short favourite, for use mainly in Lancashire, is as follows:

Question: 'What is the difference between a Yorkshireman and a coconut?'

Answer: 'You can get a drink out of one but not out of the other.'

Leo McKern

Actor (as, inter alia, 'Rumpole of the Bailey')

I must say at once that I never make after-dinner speeches; I don't make public appearances, other than those connected with my work and the necessary attendant publicity displays.

At the risk of appearing churlish, I am constantly declining kind invitations, usually from Law Societies and the like organisations who consider the man and the actor portraying a popular character one and the same, and who assume that they can rely on a good twenty minutes of Rumpolean entertainment.

Alas, I am unfortunately un-gifted in this respect – John Mortimer is really their man; although I admire and often envy those professionals who are accomplished in both fields.

I believe that the best account possible will come to nothing, however, if the narrator's personality and accomplishments are better suited to accountancy rather than an account; that personality is the thing, and that no amount of instruction or example can create one.

Also, the senses of timing and rhythm are unteachable, although should they exist, they can be polished; the dancer can fence or perform on the diving-board should he wish to do so, for he possesses gifts that are part of him (or her, of course). And if such are truly honest with themselves, they cannot even be proud of such possessions; one can pride oneself on personal accomplishment, but not on something freely given.

I am a good actor, but a very poor public speaker, which is not the paradox it sounds; as a public speaker I am exposed to the public as myself, and while I have no doubts about my abilities as an actor, I am not willy-nilly as confident as myself, for, like many of my profession, I prefer to hide behind another's mask.

The actor is not a true artist, for he or she depends on the works of others – without their writing he is nothing – and before Marcel Marceau's pierrot springs to mind, let me say he is more truly a dancer than an actor, for it is to the origins of the dance that mime owes itself.

I recall a brilliant after-dinner speaker in Australia at a Rotary dinner during the Shakespeare Memorial Theatre tour of 1953–4, and who afterwards impressed me equally at a function hosted by the English Speaking Union, when he stated his conviction that Shakespeare's plays were written not by Bacon or any other academic-sponsored possible, but by another man with the same name. A wonderful performance; in conversation with him it transpired that his main income was derived from this activity; he deserved every penny.

Of course, a speaker used to presentation of ideas, argument or reportage should be able to make a fair fist of such a speech, primed with some good material; for publicly addressing others, often critical, is a regular occurrence. But the actor left to his own devices regarding material will not necessarily make a good public speaker.

So that, alas, your reasonable request leaves me bereft of your requirements; although I know some very good stories indeed, told with success in a friendly gathering, I find after consideration (and with mild dismay) that they would be hardly suitable for a formal occasion.

I regret, therefore, that I am unable to accept your kind invitation to take part in your wholly laudable project with a reasonable contribution.

Unless, of course, you would consider this letter as such?

Sir David McNee

Q.P.M., F.B.I.M., C.St.J.

Commissioner, Metropolitan Police 1977–82

I have always found that the best stories are those told against yourself or your profession. One I have enjoyed telling, and I think audiences over the years have enjoyed listening to, runs as follows:

When I was Commissioner for Police I was invited to address a variety of audiences. I am reminded of an occasion, today, when I was asked to speak to the patients and staff of a large psychiatric hospital on the problems of policing London. I don't know why I should be reminded of that event now – it must be the decor.

Throughout my speech I was regularly interrupted by an elderly patient sitting in the front row who kept muttering 'Rubbish! Rubbish! Rubbish!' Public speaking is not easy at the best of times, but when a member of your front row audience keeps on muttering 'Rubbish! Rubbish! Rubbish!' it becomes doubly difficult.

I put up with this for about ten minutes – which is pretty good by my standards – and then turned to the consultant psychiatrist and said, 'Look, I realise you have a problem patient here; would you like me to stop for a few moments while you get him back to the ward?'

Without a moment's hesitation, the consultant replied, 'No, please continue, Sir David, Jimmy has been with us for over twenty years and this is the first time he has said anything that makes sense.'

Professor the Revd. J. Mahoney

S.J., M.A., D.D., F.R.S.A.

Department of Theology, King's College London

Your Co-operation is Requested

A close-fisted small businessman in the North of Scotland had fallen on hard times, and his creditors were increasingly insistent that he meet their demands. After trying to ease his situation in various ways, without success, he learned of a major lottery which was soon to take place. And despite his religious scruples, he decided there was nothing else for it. 'O Lord,' he prayed, 'help me win the raffle.'

As the day of the draw approached, and his debts loomed ever larger, he redoubled his prayers and begged on his knees in increasing desperation, 'Lordie, Lordie. O help me win the raffle.' And finally, a voice came from heaven, in exasperated reply: 'Angus! Meet me half-way. Buy a ticket!'

The Rt. Hon. John Major

M.P., P.C.

Prime Minister, 1990–

I have not played cricket since I injured my leg in a very serious car crash in Nigeria in the 1960s and I have found over the past two or three years that people will sometimes say extraordinary things to me that would not previously have happened. Mystics appear to predict all sorts of strange events in the future and re-write elements of the past. A mystic once explained to me apologetically, very apologetically, that my car accident had been a mistake. 'It should have happened to the car in front,' she said. I was not quite sure how to reply to that. I said to her: 'Can fate put my leg back together again?' 'Much too difficult,' said the mystic, 'leg broken, ligaments torn, kneecap smashed, not a hope of putting it together again. But I can probably give you a wish as a consolation prize.' 'Excellent,' I said. 'Please spare us an England middle order collapse in the next test match.' She paused and said: 'Well let me have another look at that leg.'

His Excellency Roy Marshall

The High Commissioner for Barbados
Former Captain of Hampshire Cricket Club

A shopkeeper in Barbados ran what you would call a corner-shop in England, which sold a variety of goods to anyone who was willing and able to buy. He was assisted by his wife and family and supported by a variety of cats which he kept ostensibly to protect his wares from the ravages of mice and the like.

On one occasion I was in the shop when a woman burst in, complaining angrily about the depredations of one of the cats which she alleged had stolen and eaten the five pounds of fish that she had purchased for her family's dinner. Without batting an eyelid, the shopkeeper pointed to a corner, where a cat was dozing contentedly, and asked: 'Lady, is that the cat?' 'Yes,' she replied, whereupon he went over, picked up the cat, brought it back to the counter and put it on the scales which weighed in at just over five pounds. 'Lady,' asked the shopkeeper, 'if that is your fish, where the hell is my cat?'

*　　　*　　　*

A racehorse trainer in Barbados put an apprentice jockey on one of his horses and took the precaution of giving him precise instructions about how to ride it. 'When you jump out of the starting stalls,' he said, 'settle the horse on the rails in second or third place, and when you come to the turn into the finishing straight the leaders will tire and roll away from the rail, leaving a gap for you to go through. Rush through the gap and keep going until you reach the winning post.' All went well as planned until the gap appeared and then, instead of going through it, the apprentice beat a hasty retreat and finished last. Upon the apprentice's return to the unsaddling enclosure, the trainer berated him for disregarding instructions; to which the apprentice calmly replied: 'Governor, have you ever tried to go through a gap that's moving faster than you?'

Dr Desmond Morris

B.Sc., D. Phil.

Author, Naturalist, Television Personality and
Broadcaster
Res. Fell., Wolfson College, Oxford

One of the most fascinating men I ever knew was the
Austrian naturalist Konrad Lorenz.

His whole life-style seemed to be an animal-infested
chaos. Like some kind of modern Noah, he lived
surrounded by fish, reptiles, birds and mammals of every
shape and colour. There were endless mishaps and it was
often from these that Lorenz learned his most valuable
lessons.

For instance, he was out walking with a tame raven
one afternoon. The bird was free-flying and, in order to
keep it close to him, Lorenz had taken the precaution of
filling one of his pockets with small pieces of raw meat.
Every so often, he would call to the bird (he was fluent in
Raven) and as it approached, would put his hand into
the meat-pocket, take out a strip of meat, and feed it to
his great, black companion. This procedure meant that,
although the raven would zoom off into the sky, it
always kept a bright, corvine eye on Konrad's
movements as he wandered across the summer fields.

They continued like this for several hours, with the
bird returning regularly to Lorenz's side for a further
titbit. As it was a hot day, Lorenz had drunk copiously at
lunch-time and now needed to relieve himself. There was
nobody about, so he moved near a hedge, undid his
trousers, and started to do so. The raven's sharp eye had
observed Lorenz undoing his trousers and assumed that
he was opening another pocket to extract a fresh piece of
meat. Swooping down with a raucous cry, the great bird
seized this new piece of meat, clamping down tightly on
it with its massive powerful beak. Lorenz let out a roar
like a wounded bull and began leaping dementedly about

in the corner of the field. The raven was nonplussed by this extraordinary behaviour and could not understand why its human friend was so reluctant to hand over a piece of meat that was so plainly meant for its consumption. Placing its huge feet firmly on Lorenz's body, the bird started to tug fiercely at the stubbornly resistant food-offering, like a blackbird trying to pull an earthworm from a garden lawn. Lorenz claims that he nearly fainted from pain and loss of blood.

Jean Muir

C.B.E., F.R.S.A., R.D.I., F.C.S.D.

Couturier, Winner of many International Awards

A recent design award, given by the French, was in the form of a ceramic sculpture by Niki de Saint Phalle and appropriate male and female forms were given – quite clearly, no one thought to tell the engraver that whilst Jean Muir in French sounded like a man's name, in English it wasn't. There was an amusing bit of veiled kerfuffle whilst the gender was changed and hastily despatched across the Channel.

Now if I had been named Douglas Malcolm Campbell Muir, as my grandmother had intended – instead of being a paltry girl – the confusion would never have arisen. (In dictating – I found that spelt 'poultry'.)

What price fame!

Emma Nicholson

M.P.

Chairman of the Duke of Edinburgh's Award Scheme
1988–

My father, Sir Godfrey Nicholson, a former Conservative
M.P., needed drastic stomach surgery several years
before he died. In Reading General Hospital he found
himself in a long ward, next to an elderly man who was
having his leg amputated – a strong Labour supporter all
his life who had never knowingly spoken to a
Conservative, on principle, in his entire life – and these
two elderly men kept each other alive by fierce political
arguments over the four-week period of their operations.

They became close friends but, despite all their efforts,
failed to involve the man in the opposite bed who would
not speak to them at all. On leaving day, all became
clear. The silent man came over and said, 'I am sorry to
have left you both entirely alone, but as Archdeacon of
Berkshire felt I really could not get involved in politics!'

Nick Owen
Television Personality and Presenter

I was in Switzerland once, when I overheard an Irishman on a skiing holiday in conversation with one of the locals.

'Can you tell me the way to the nearest ski-slope?'

'Sorry,' came the reply. 'I'm a tobogganist.'

'Oh, in that case,' said the Irishman, 'I'll have twenty Benson and Hedges.'

Jill Parkin

Chief Feature Writer, *Daily Express*

You can fall down flat on your face in journalism, in front of a circulation-sized audience. It's because of the need to become an instant expert on something, whether it's Hezbollah or the nation's divorce law. Or, in my case, cakes.

Normally, you see, you ring up the experts and say, 'What do you think of this hostage deal, then?' or 'What effect will the new law have on our children?' And they tell you, and you tell the readers. And for a few hours you're an expert on whatever it is, and then you forget about it and become as ignorant as you were before.

But when I was given half the women's page of the *Harrogate Advertiser* to write at the age of 21, I didn't have to ring anyone. It was coming up to bonfire night and, with a name like mine, what could be better than to give the readers a recipe for parkin? Do you know what parkin is? It's a sticky, dark, oaty cake which you keep for a few days before cutting up and eating around the bonfire.

So in went the recipe, copied from a family book and blessed with the authority of my surname.

'Do come round and try the parkin I made from your recipe,' a reader rang up to say. A friendly lot they are in Harrogate, and I didn't have much to do that afternoon. I wasn't at all suspicious.

The parkin sat on her kitchen table, a knife immovably stuck in it. 'It's not right, is it?' said the reader. Perhaps she was expecting a light ginger sponge, I muttered. Parkin wasn't like that.

Parkin wasn't like this, either. A shattered edge showed where someone had bravely sampled it. It looked as if it had been pebble-dashed. I was allowed out alive.

My mother, who had never tried the recipe herself, reckoned there was something like three times too great a weight of oats in it. In Harrogate I have yet to live it down.

Michael Parkinson
Television and Radio Personality and Chat Show Host

To sit, for example, in the presence of Dame Edith Evans was to be enriched by the energy, intelligence and humour of one unique soul. She taught me more about the proper conduct of the public figure than anyone. She would arrive at the show resplendent in fur coat, new dress by Norman Hartnell, and a large Rolls-Royce. Immediately, she would button-hole anyone within reach and complain about the parlous state of the old age pensioner.

The third occasion this happened, I felt confident enough to challenge her. I said that her argument would carry a lot more force were she not so obviously glamorous and successful. I should have known better. 'What do you mean?' she asked in that regal voice. 'Well,' I said, 'you can't really stand as an advocate for old age pensioners when you arrive in a fur coat and a new frock by Mr. Hartnell.' She looked at me with chilling disdain. I should have read the warning signs, but I pressed on. 'What is more,' I said, 'you can't complain about the pension when you drive up in a Rolls.' 'My dear boy,' she retorted, 'would you suggest that I arrive in a Mini?' Of course not. She was a star and she knew that the public wanted her to fulfil their expectations of style and glamour.

She remained a star to her dying day because she understood her obligation. When she was very ill, her friend and biographer Bryan Forbes prepared his young daughter for the inevitable bad news. The child said: 'But she won't die, will she? She's not the type.'

Maureen Paton

Daily Express Drama Critic

Henry and the Art of Ham Dram

There was a very sad case with a touch of theatrical bravura at one of our minor criminal courts recently. The subject of our story is a mummer called Henry.

Henry is an actor with deep commitment, limited abilities and less luck. Though in his young days – a long time ago – he was handsome, the ravages of thespian life had left him with the look of a raddled St. Bernard whose jowls grazed the ground. He therefore decided to specialise in notable character parts like Fagin, Richard III and the Hunchback of Notre Dame.

But when he writhed around at auditions, twisted back his shoulder and began: 'Now is the winter . . .' the casting director would say, 'No, no Larry imitations, if you don't mind. What else can you do?' So he would grimace, stick his tongue in his cheek and quaver: 'The bells . . .' only to be interrupted by cries of, 'No, no, not another Charles Laughton take-off!'

Poor Henry lost his confidence and lapsed into the worst excesses of amateur dramatics, better known as Ham-Dram in the business.

The only letters he received were reminders that his electricity/tax/rent/suit-hire accounts were overdue. Threats followed. He took to haunting certain theatrical pubs, partly in the hope of meeting someone who might offer him a starring role and partly to accept a small loan or a large drink offered by a reluctant listener to his tales of woe.

Late one evening, a particularly flamboyant theatrical agent swept into the pub and bumped against him. 'Sorry, old man,' sneered the agent. 'Didn't see you there – but then nobody ever sees you anywhere, do they? How's the Ham-Dram?'

Henry, somewhat the worse for several large whiskies, could not remember much else. The following morning he discovered that he had stolen the agent's wallet. It was an old trick he had learned when doing two weeks as Fagin in Scunthorpe several years ago. He liked to keep his hand in; but this was ridiculous.

There were two final demands on the table. Perhaps he could pay these off with the money from the wallet and return the cash anonymously when his luck changed. Thus began Henry's life of crime. He persuaded himself that there was a precedent in Shakespeare with Iago's advice: 'Put money in thy purse.' He chose his victims with care. They had to be rude, pompous, stingy, arrogant and rich. A lot of them were theatrical agents.

To be just to Henry, he hated his new occupation. After every pick-pocketing expedition, he would return home racked with guilt and with stern vows on his lips never to take another wallet. Months passed, and so did all the good character roles to other less worthy actors. Poor Henry longed to orate, pronounce, denounce, wickedly laugh, sneeringly sneer, conspire and expire in full view of an appreciative audience. He would even settle for a nice little car commercial instead of King Lear. Yet here he was, having to sidle unnoticed through an ungrateful crowd that would never appreciate his performance.

One day in Oxford Street, his own pocket was picked as he waited at a bus stop. 'Oh, the bitter irony,' I hear you say. You should have heard Henry. A trio of burly detectives – one of whom was disguised as a bag-lady – leaped on the thief. They were like buses – they always came in threes. 'You'll have to come to the station, sir, to identify the contents of your wallet,' said a cop to Henry, who blushed, stammered, hesitated and forgot his lines.

The contents of his wallet were highly incriminating, containing a large number of other people's credit cards. After listening to the evidence, the beak leaned towards Henry and asked: 'How could a man like you, belonging to an honourable profession numbering many knights of the realm among its ranks, stoop to this unnatural behaviour and develop the arcane skill to carry out your nefarious activities?'

Henry was suddenly visited by a ghastly vision of those brown envelopes floating through his letter-box, each one screaming, 'Pay, pay or else there'll be hell to pay.' He twisted back his shoulder, half-crouched, swung his left arm, violently grimaced and, in a Ham-Dram voice that smote the ears of his appreciative audience, declared: 'It was the bills, the bills, that made me deft!'

The Rt. Hon. Christopher Patten

P.C.

Former Chairman of the Conservative Party
H.M. Governor of Hong Kong 1992–

I am slowly growing accustomed to being recognised by
the public, but it sometimes takes a bizarre form. Coming
back from holiday on the ferry last year, after a good deal
of nudging from his wife, a man came across to me and
said, 'You must get fed up with people saying this to
you.' 'Saying what?' I replied nervously. 'How like Chris
Patten you look,' he went on.

Jeremy Paxman
Presenter of BBC 2 'Newsnight'

One day I was interviewing a trade union leader about an industrial dispute. 'What's this strike really about, Mr. Kennedy?' I asked.

He looked blank. I asked him again: 'What's this strike REALLY about, Mr. Kennedy?'

He looked bewildered. The third time I tried again, spelling the words out very slowly indeed. 'What . . . is . . . this . . . strike . . . about?'

Finally came the reply: 'Search me – my name's Johnson.'

Sir Peter Saunders

Producer of the world's longest running play, *The Mousetrap*
Former Film Director and Journalist

Agatha Christie's *The Mousetrap* is not allowed to be produced in Great Britain except for the West End production, and one day a press cutting mentioned that it was to be performed by a school.

My agents contacted the Headmaster, who said they hadn't realised the embargo, and he wrote to me asking for it to be lifted.

I wrote back and said that regretfully any exception to the ban could lead to the opening of floodgates and, sadly, I couldn't make an exception for him.

He wrote back a charming letter saying he quite understood, but his production would not have interfered with mine because he had intended re-writing it.

The Rt. Hon. Nicholas Scott

M.B.E., M.P.

National President of Tory Reform Group
Minister for Social Security and Disabled People

Two judges were driving back towards the south-west of Ireland from a long and heavy Bar dinner in Dublin. At about two o'clock in the morning they felt that the alcohol in their systems had receded to a dangerously low level and, seeing a member of the Irish Police standing in the corner of a small town they were passing through, pulled over and enquired whether he knew of a place where two thirsty men might get a drink at that time in the morning. After much pondering, the Guard confessed he did not know anywhere in the town where two thirsty men might get a drink at that hour of the morning; but on reflection, he did just know where *three* thirsty men could obtain the same objective.

*   *   *

Finding that his bicycle was missing, the vicar decided he would lecture his parishioners not simply to obey the Commandment 'Thou shalt not steal,' but to go through each and every one of the Ten Commandments, exhorting them to obey rules in letter and in spirit. And he was in fine form! After the service the curate went over to congratulate him, but added that the vicar had seemed to lose his way a little bit when he got to 'Thou shalt not commit adultery'. 'Yes, I am sorry about that,' said the vicar, 'but I suddenly remembered where I had left my bicycle.'

Selina Scott

Television Personality
Presenter of *The Clothes Show*

As a young 'celebrity' on a local TV station in Aberdeen, I was stopped by a woman in Union Street, who was insistent: 'I know your face,' she said.

I stopped and smiled, and waited for her to say, 'I've got it, you're Selina Scott who presents "North Tonight" . . .'

Instead, she came out with: 'I've got it, you're the lassie who serves behind the counter in the Co-Op butchers in Mastrick.'

His Excellency R. G. H. Seitz
Ambassador of the United States of America

The Civil War is one of the great defining events in American history. Oscar Wilde became aware of this fact during his first lecture tour in the United States. As part of his travels, he visited Charleston, South Carolina, known as the birthplace of the Confederacy. After dinner one evening, he walked on to the porch to catch the cooling breeze from Charleston Harbour and to admire the scenery of the moonlit night. As he enjoyed the evening air, he was joined by another guest, a Charlestonian. Looking for conversation, Wilde glanced up to the sky and commented, 'Isn't the moon beautiful tonight?' His companion paused a moment, sighed and replied, 'Ah, yes, but you should have seen it before the war.'

This is one of the few recorded moments in which Oscar Wilde was left speechless.

Dinah Sheridan
Star of Stage and Screen and Television Personality

My favourite poem:

> I'm used to my arthritis,
> To my dentures I'm resigned,
> I can cope with my bi-focals,
> But Oh God! I miss my mind!

Ned Sherrin

M.A.

Barrister
Producer, Director, Presenter and Writer in Cinema,
Theatre, Radio and Television

This is one of my favourite after-dinner anecdotes, but so
many people now know it that I can't use it any more! It
is also said to be highly popular with the Duchess of
York.

It is the sad story of the man told by his doctor that he
has less than 24 hours to live. He goes home and breaks
the news to his wife. Loyally she plans to give him the
perfect dying hours. She suggests a theatre visit to see
his favourite star. He says, no, he couldn't face that. She
tries tempting him with his favourite restaurant. No, he
does not fancy that. Desperate, she offers to drive him to
their much loved favourite beauty spot, hold hands and
look up at the stars. This fails too.

She give him the responsibility. What would he like to
do? He says he wants to take a case of champagne up to
the bedroom and make love all night.

'That's OK for you,' she says. 'You don't have to get
up in the morning.'

David Shilling,
Hat Designer and Author

I very seldom agree to give after-dinner speeches myself, and so there haven't been many hilarious results or calamities. But years ago I was asked up North to a Ladies' Dinner Club with a fine reputation for excellent speakers, and they'd just had the actor Donald Sinden, whose family I know.

I'm sure the meal was delicious but I was too expectant to enjoy it, and then Madame Chairman was on her feet. She may have started with 'our guest who needs no further introduction', but she wasn't prepared to leave it at that. As I played nervously with the DS jewelled initialled hat pin I had laid in front of me, she carried on . . . and on . . . After the first twenty minutes or so, she was leaving me with not much left to say, but by now many in the audience were asleep, so why worry! But it was her last two words that actually left me absolutely speechless: 'and now I want you to give a warm welcome to . . .' She hesitated, and perhaps she was looking at the 'DS' pin in my hand. '. . . Donald Sinden!'

At least it woke the audience, but I haven't been back.

Tommy Steele

O.B.E.

Stage and Film Actor, and Author

I was having dinner at the Kremlin in Moscow in 1957
and I had to propose a toast in the name of the youth of
our two great nations – it ended with me saying 'and the
best of British Luck'.

Comrade Mikoyan (later the Russian President) refused
to accept that only the British had luck.

I countered that only the British deserved it! There was
some laughter and a lot of long faces.

I presumed that the Russians do not have a lot of
humour.

Alastair Stewart
Television News Reader

Three academics – a physicist, an engineer and an economist – are shipwrecked on a desert island with only a can of beans to sustain them but no means of opening it.

The physicist says: 'If we leave it in the sun, the rays will heat and expand the air inside and blow the lid off. Then we can eat the beans.'

The engineer says: 'No, the beans will go everywhere. Let us construct an umbrella from palm leaves, place the can in the up-turned umbrella and then, when the effect of the sun's rays blows the lid off, we can catch the beans and then eat them.'

They both turn to the economist, who thinks for a moment and then says: 'Let us ASSUME we have a can-opener . . .'

Dr. Miriam Stoppard

M.D., M.R.C.P.

Television Personality, Author and Journalist

This is true, and it's an after-lunch party:

H.R.H. Prince Philip's 70th birthday lunch, with 300 women from the National Playing Fields Association, of which he is President.

We all stand for the loyal toast. We all raise our glasses to the Queen and, as we sit down, he says: 'I say, it's getting a bit feminist around here!'

The Reverend Canon Richard Tydeman

M.A.

Canon of St. Paul's Cathedral 1963–81
Preacher to Lincoln's Inn 1972–81
Frequent contributor to BBC Drama

Most of the stories which I have *told* are stories which I
have *heard*, and therefore I cannot claim 'authorship'.
However, you might like to make use of the following
incidents which I can guarantee are all absolutely true.

My Favourite Wedding Story

I had been conducting a wedding rehearsal in Church
with the bride and groom, going through the service and
answering questions. The couple were just leaving
afterwards, when the groom came back. 'By the way,' he
said, 'will you put the word "obey" in the bride's
promise?' 'Well,' I said, 'we usually omit it nowadays,
but of course I will put it in if you want it.' 'Oh,' said the
groom, 'I'm not bothered myself; but she wants it put in,
and I always do what she says.'

My Favourite Funeral Story

I was visiting an old lady on the anniversary of her
husband's death. 'I had him cremated you know,' she
said. 'Yes,' I replied, 'I think cremation is a very good
thing, don't you?' 'Indeed I do,' she said, 'And I have
decided to be cremated myself – if I'm spared.'

My Favourite Radio Story

Shortly after the war, while things were still scarce, I
happened to come in one day when my wife was
listening to 'Woman's Hour', and heard the lady
announcer say, 'I am glad to tell you that corsets are

coming back in the shops at last, but at present only in the smaller sizes. We larger women will have to go on looking round for a while.'

Carol Vorderman
Statistician and Television Personality in *Countdown*

One day we were recording 'Countdown' in the
Yorkshire Television studios in Leeds, and on that day
Ned Sherrin was the guest celebrity in Dictionary Corner.
As we were walking out of the studio at the end of one of
the programmes, I started chatting to Ned about *Ziegfeld*
which had recently opened in the West End. I was going
on about the disappointing reviews and how unkind the
critics had been to the show. Ned turned to me and said,
'Well, it will be interesting to see what Tommy Steele
does to the production.' (Tommy had just been brought
in as director.) I said, 'Yes, he certainly can't do any
worse than they've done already. By the way, Ned, have
you seen it yet?' Ned loomed over me with his six foot
three frame, looked me straight in the eye and said, 'Yes
darling, I wrote it.' Ouch!

The Rt. Hon. Lord Wakeham

P.C., J.P., F.C.A.

Lord President of the Council and Leader of The House
of Commons 1987–88
Former Secretary of State for Energy
Minister of State for the Treasury 1982–83
Leader of the House of Lords 1992–

They say that 'once bitten, twice shy'.

With that maxim firmly in mind, I always approach the
task of recollecting stories and anecdotes with a great
deal of both reluctance and trepidation. And the reason
for that is that many years ago I was asked to pen two
amusing jokes for a collection of stories, in aid of another
very worthy project.

As any true politician would, I decided to keep the best
jokes to myself and not make them available to all and
sundry. So I recounted two of the worst jokes I knew –
jokes which NEVER raised a laugh when I told them.

You can therefore imagine my humiliation when – a
number of years later – I attended a very grand dinner
and the host began his speech of introduction with those
very same jokes I had surrendered to the book. But
instead of the stony silence I had always received in
telling them, his audience erupted into howls of laughter.

From that moment on, I decided that discretion is the
better part of valour and to keep EVERY joke for myself.

Montague Waters

Q.C.

Eskimos are known for their taciturnity. Two of them
were in a boat fishing for several hours, without success.
Not a word passed between them. Suddenly, one felt a
tug on his line and, after a short tussle, he landed his
catch – a beautiful mermaid. After a while – and whilst
his companion watched, expressionless – he grasped the
mermaid and threw her back into the water.

An hour passed, and then his companion said: 'Why?'
After a lengthy pause, he replied, 'How?'

The Rt. Hon. Bernard Weatherill

P.C.

Former Speaker of the House of Commons

Out of the Mouths!

When Margaret Thatcher was Prime Minister, we were joined in Speaker's House for a family Christmas in 1989 by eight of our grandchildren. Before the meal I overheard this conversation:

James (aged 6): 'If we're going to play Parliament, I don't see why I should have to be Grandpa again!'

Julia (aged 7),
his cousin: 'Well, you can't be the Prime Minister anyway, 'cos only *girls* can be Prime Minister, silly!'

Richard Whiteley
Presenter of Channel 4's *Countdown*

Years ago, as a young TV reporter, I was interviewing a farmer on the wilder uplands of Wensleydale. After the interview, about the hardships of hill farming, I was conscious of the time and of having to get the film crew off for their lunch.

Not having a watch that day for some reason, I asked the farmer for the time.

'Aye, lad,' he said. 'Ah'll tell thee.' He crouched down beside the cow in the farmyard and, with his great Yorkshire horny hand, strengthened and pitted with years of toil, lifted the cow's udder ever so gently.

'Ten to one,' was the reply.

The film crew and I were amazed.

'How can you tell the time by feeling a cow's udder?' I marvelled.

'Come here, lad, ah'll show thee.' Stooping down again, he said, 'If you crouch down like this and lift up the udder, you can just see the church clock across the valley.'

June Whitfield
O.B.E.

Actress and Television Personality

A very boring speaker had been droning on for 45 minutes; some of his audience had closed their eyes, when he was heard to say: 'I speak not only for this generation, but for generations to come . . .'

From the back of the hall came the shout: 'If you don't hurry up – they'll all be here!'

Ernie Wise

O.B.E.

Comedian and Television Personality

Boxer: 'I would like to fight George Foreman.'
Manager: 'Don't be silly, he will kill you.'
Boxer: 'All right, what about Mike Tyson?'
Manager: 'No way, he's too experienced, he would murder you.'
Boxer: 'All right, what about Frank Bruno?'
Manager: 'Don't be daft, you are Frank Bruno.'

*　　*　　*

Woman walking round London Zoo, when a gorilla grabbed her.

She shouted to her husband: 'Save me, I think he's going to make love to me.'

The husband shouts: 'Tell him you've got a headache, like you tell me.'

Other Titles from Piatkus Books

If you have enjoyed *100 Best After-Dinner Stories* you may be interested in other books published by Piatkus for after-dinner speakers and communicators. Titles include:

All in a Day's Work: A Wealth of Witty After-Dinner Anecdotes from the Famous Mark Hornsby

Confident Conversation: How to Talk in Any Business or Social Situation Dr. Lillian Glass

It Gives Me Great Pleasure: The Complete After-Dinner Speaker's Handbook Herbert Prochnow

My Lords, Ladies and Gentlemen: The Best and Funniest After-Dinner Stories from the Famous Phyllis Shindler

Powerspeak: The Complete Guide to Public Speaking and Communication Dorothy Leeds

The Power Talk System: How to Communicate Effectively Christian H. Godefroy and Stephanie Barrat

Raise Your Glasses: The Best and Wittiest Anecdotes and After-Dinner Stories from the Famous Phyllis Shindler

For a free brochure with further information on our range of titles, please write to:

Piatkus Books
Freepost 7 (WD 4505)
London, W1E 4EZ